THIS LITTLE TIGER BOOK
BELONGS TO.

_____

_____

To all the little squids that
feel wobbly sometimes
~ W M

For Lauren and Elliott
~ D B

LITTLE TIGER PRESS LTD,
an imprint of the Little Tiger Group
1 Coda Studios, 189 Munster Road, London SW6 6AW
www.littletiger.co.uk

First published in Great Britain 2019
This edition published 2020

Printed in China • LTP/1400/3057/1219

2 4 6 8 10 9 7 5 3 1

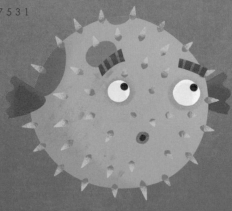

Supported using public funding by
ARTS COUNCIL
ENGLAND

WENDY MEDDOUR

DUNCAN BEEDIE

STEFANO THE SQUID
HERO OF THE DEEP

LITTLE TIGER

LONDON

There is one thing everyone should know about the sea:

BEING A SQUID

ISN'T EASY.

Stefano found it very difficult indeed.

You see, all the other creatures in
the ocean were amazing:
there were clever dolphins that could leap out
of the waves, carpet sharks that could hide
on the ocean floor, and pufferfish that could
blow up like balloons.

The *Deep Sea TV*
team *always* filmed them.
They never filmed Stefano.

"Why don't they like me?" asked Stefano.

"Because you're not very colourful," said the parrotfish.

"And you're not very bat-like," bubbled the batfish.

"And you don't look like a hammer," said the hammerhead shark.

"That's because I'm a squid," sighed Stefano.

"Well, try and look more intelligent,"
squeaked the dolphins.
"Try and look more leafy,"
flapped the leafy sea dragon.
"Or try and look more like a vegetable?"
suggested the sea cucumber.

"I can't!" said Stefano.
"I'm a *squid!*"

"Have you got a deadly weapon?"
sneered an anglerfish.
"N-n-no," stuttered Stefano, trying his
best to swim away.

Stefano wobbled off and hid in a cave.
Some divers swam past with their cameras.
No wonder they didn't want to film him.

"Don't be sad," said Sea Cucumber.
"We can't all look like a vegetable.
At least you're good at being a squid."

Just then, a GIANT squid floated past.

The limpets stared at its massive suckers.
Then they stared at Stefano.
"You're not very big, are you?" they said.

Stefano blushed.
"I'm a c-c-common
squid," he said.
"I'm supposed to be
this small."

"Never mind that!!" cried Sea Cucumber.
"Look! There's a diver in trouble."

One of the crew had
got left behind.
"He's running out of air,"
said the pufferfish.

"Someone do something!" shouted Sea Cucumber.
No one moved.
"Stefano! Do something!" she shrieked again.

"But I'm just a common squid," said Stefano.
"It doesn't matter what you are," said Sea Cucumber.
"That diver needs your help."

Stefano gulped and a **big puff**
of black ink came out of his bottom!

But he didn't let that stop him.

Stefano swam over to the diver
as fast as he could.

Bubbles were pouring out
of the diver's tank!

Suddenly, Stefano had an idea.

He shoved one of his suckers over the hole.
The bubbles stopped!

"HOORAY!" cheered Sea Cucumber. "YOU DID IT!"
Stefano beamed.

Safely back on board
the boat, the diver took
off his mask and blew
Stefano and Sea Cucumber
a kiss. Stefano gasped.

The diver wasn't a 'he'. It was the one and only
Henrietta Fierce: the presenter of *Deep Sea TV!*

"She doesn't look as clever as me," said the dolphin.
"Or as colourful as me," said the parrotfish.
"Or as batty as me," burped the batfish.

Stefano and Sea Cucumber
just blushed.

The next day, Henrietta Fierce and her film crew
came back with all their cameras and lights.
"Over here," shouted the carpet shark.
"I'M the star of the show."
"Don't be silly. I AM!" squealed a starfish.

"Move aside," growled the anglerfish.
"They've come to film ME."
But they hadn't. Of course they hadn't.
Can you guess who they'd come to film?
That's right . . .

STEFANO AND SEA CUCUMBER: AMAZING SUPERHEROES OF THE DEEP!
ROLL 6
TAKE 2
SCENE 14

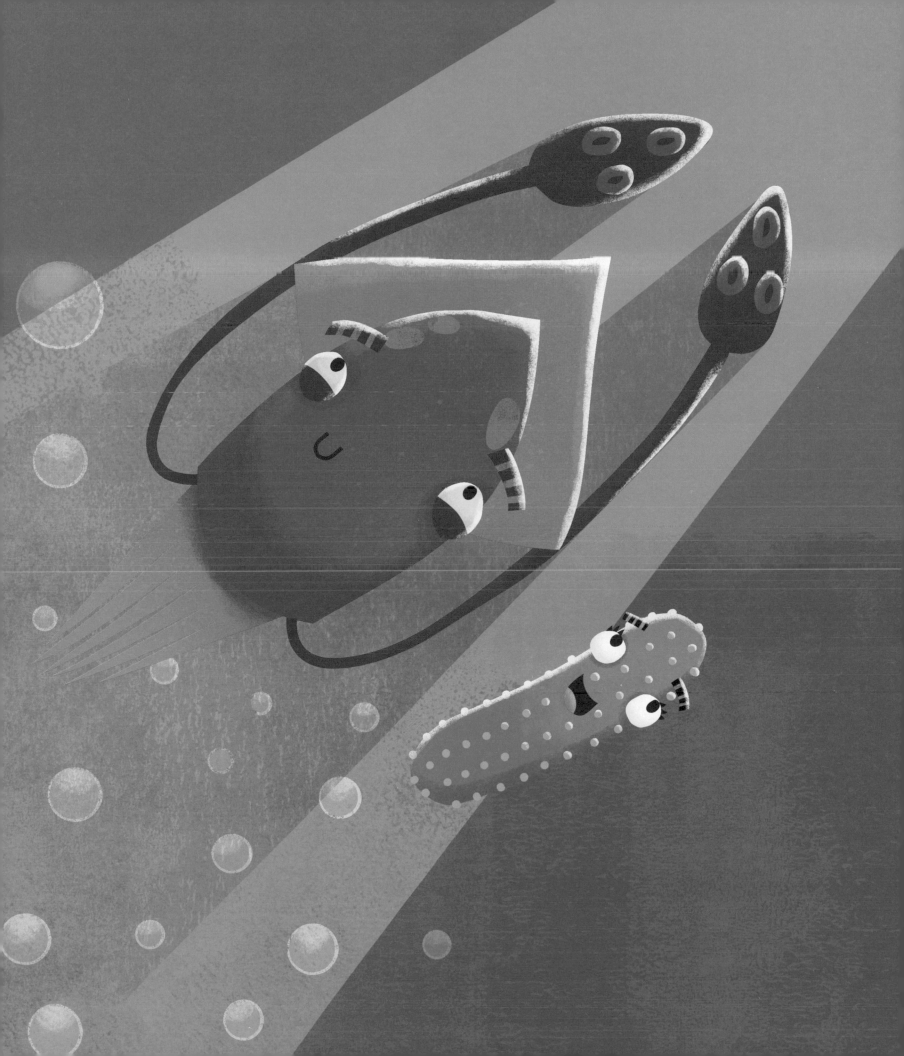

DIVE INTO MORE ADVENTURES WITH LITTLE TIGER . . .

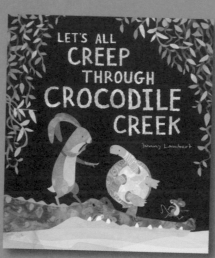

OCTOPANTS

SUZY SENIOR

CLAIRE POWELL

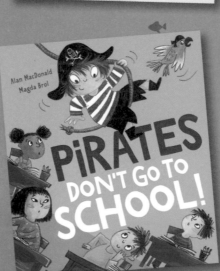

LET'S ALL CREEP THROUGH CROCODILE CREEK

Jenny Lambert

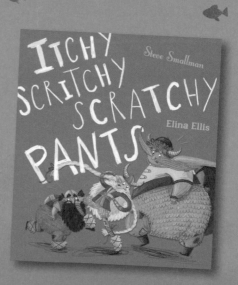

the SPACE TRAIN

Maudie Powell-Tuck · Karl James Mountford

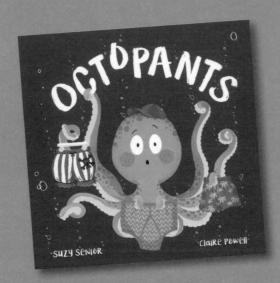

Tracey Corderoy

Tony Neal

THE ONE-STOP STORY SHOP

Alan MacDonald

Magda Brol

PIRATES DON'T GO TO SCHOOL!

Steve Smallman

ITCHY SCRITCHY SCRATCHY PANTS

Elina Ellis

LITTLE TIGER

For information regarding any of the above titles or for our catalogue, please contact us:
Little Tiger Press Ltd, 1 Coda Studios, 189 Munster Road, London SW6 6AW
Tel: 020 7385 6333 • E-mail: contact@littletiger.co.uk • www.littletiger.co.uk